RESILIENCE

DE-CLASSIFIED

SPUNDAN DASGUPTA

Contents

DEFECTED

"Are you sure about this? Won't we get caught?" Asked Shriya.

Ajesh looked out of the window checking for anyone watching or spying over them. He then looked at Shiya and answered, "We have been planning this for months. We cannot fail now. And God forbid, if we are caught... they better kill us for I am not going back to those sinners."

Shriya checked their bags again and once she was satisfied that everything necessary was taken, she got up from the bed and walked towards Ajesh.

"You call them sinners but... we were a part of it for 5 years. We have committed sins. I hope we do not pay the price for it after so much planning." Said Shriya, feeling concerned.

Ajesh understood what Shriya was talking about. They were a member of the Nationalist Corp but in the eyes of BASE, they were anti-nationals. However, recent events in their faction have led them to take a drastic step to go rogue and seek the help of BASE to save them.

"Yes, we have sinned and this is our first big step for redemption. Either we will be forgiven or punished. Whatever be the outcome, our job is clear. BASE needs to know who they are fighting. For them, the nationalist corp is still an unknown army.

This army hides a dark secret which if unleashed can result in the end of humanity itself... and no way, I am allowing that. We have been fed lies and now... we need to make them repent for their actions." Said Ajesh.

There is a hard knock on the door and the duo is alarmed by it.

"Open up, it is me, Darshan." Darshan spoke up as he knocked on the door again.

Ajesh signaled Shriya to stand back while brandishing his sidearm. Slowly, he opened the door and looked outside. It was Darshan but Ajesh still checked if there is anybody else.

"Come on, pal. So many years together yet you don't believe me. What kind of a friend are you?" Darshan asks in a sarcastic tone.

"Don't throw your sarcasm bullshit at me. These are tough times and we cannot believe anyone unknown. You, however, my friend, have been gone for a long time. We need to move now so you better give me some good news." Ajesh said in an exasperated tone.

"We needed transportation to reach the location those officials stated... and I have got that. A rusty old car but it will do." Said Darshan.

"Rusty old car, eh! Yeah, it will do. Shriya, grab the stuffs. Let us get out of here." Said Ajesh.

"Those officials, I hope they will be here. I hope they will believe why we contacted them. We have not planned all this shit to be caught again and be executed." Said Darshan.

"Just stay positive and stick to whatever we have planned. If we have to fight to get to the target location, then we will fight to our last breath. As for those officials, we have juicy information... information that they have always been looking for. Oh, they will come. They will risk their lives for it." said Ajesh.

The trio came out of the house and walked downstairs looking here and there for any suspicious person or thing tracking them.

"We should have covered our face to avoid detection." Said Shriya.

"No, that is a bad idea. Ironically, our covers will be blown if we cover ourselves. Behave normally and no one will spot us." said Ajesh.

They reached the car. Darshan moved forward, took out the car keys and opened the door of the driver's seat.

"You call this a car. This looks like... all the pieces would come out in a jiffy if you just touch it." said Ajesh.

"You are overreacting. This is a used BASE car, officials used it 20 years ago till they brought out something sturdier. Considering it is a BASE car, they don't sell well even in the black market. Not even for scrap. Whoever had this just wanted to do away with it, so I paid 200 credits for this." Darshan responded.

The trio got into the car, Darshan started the engines and drove through the busy streets.

"Guess not all glitters are gold. Still, this is a good enough ride. Well done, Darshan. Let us get to target location." Said Ajesh.

Both Ajesh and Darshan switched on their GPRS to look for the safest way to reach the location.

"Should we contact the officials now?" Asked Shriya.

"Only when we are out of the city. As long as we are in the city, we will tracked." Ajesh responded.

Darshan glanced at the side mirror, he spotted something and he wasn't happy about it.

"Guys, we are been followed." Darshan said.

"You don't say." Ajesh reacted and looked back.

Indeed, 2 SUVs were following them.

"Yes, they are following us. The question is, what are they waiting for? Why aren't they firing at us?" Asked Ajesh.

"Oh really! You want them to fire at us. Let us do one thing, let us stop the car and ask them as when they are going to fire at us." Said Darshan.

Ajesh scowled at Darshan. He was about to answer when suddenly, the miniguns on the SUVs started to fire at them.

"There, you got your answer. Don't worry, this car is old but BASE material. It will hold." Said Darshan.

That very moment, the side view mirror was shattered due to the minigun fire.

"Yeah well, only for a short time." Darshan commented.

"Lousy bastards! Shriya, open the bag and take out the assault rifles. They want a fight; we will gladly give them." Said Ajesh and

Shriya did the same.

Brandishing them, they duo started to fire while Darshan concentrated on the road. The vehicles were going through a bustling street and with the firing in progress, people were either looking for cover or trying to run. A few unfortunate souls were caught in the crossfire with the miniguns brutally killing and tearing them to pieces.

"This is bad. Those poor people... Darshan, you need to get off this road. Find another path or more will die." Said a concerned Shriya.

"I am trying, Shriya but there is nothing we can do for them." Darshan replied.

"Ajesh to BASE command, please respond. We are under heavy fire. Seeking assistance. Please respond. Please respond. Over." Ajesh got on the radio signaling for help.

45 minutes earlier

"Being a leader is tough task, isn't it?" Jenny asked.

"You have no idea but why do you ask?" Shekhar responded while still busy filing a report.

"It is Karan. He has been too busy lately. I know we are soldiers. Free time is a luxury for us but even when we get that, Karan... he always finds something else to do." Jenny said looking morose and staring at the roof.

"Aww, ain't that cute!" Shekhar commented with a chuckle.

"Oh, come one, Shekhar! I am serious." Said Jenny.

Shekhar saved the report and then emailed it. Switching off the computer, he turned towards Jenny and with a smile, said, "Karan never really believed that one day he will be a leader. He was always filled with doubts. Will it surprise you by saying that Karan was in two minds actually to join BASE?"

Jenny was not surprised; she was shocked and alarmed.

"I don't believe it. You are talking about the same man who 2 years ago led us in destroying that pyramid. Nowhere did I make out that he would be in-confident about being a soldier." Said Jenny.

"Hmmm, that is only because... he is a man who thrives on crisis." Shekhar responded and Jenny stared at him wanting to know more.

Shekhar continued, "In my days in school, I was a last bencher. Either I never did my homework or submitted them late. Fun and frolic were my 'philosophy'. I was in my 5th grade when Karan joined my school. Silent, studious and always keeping himself away from any drama. Being the new student, I, along with my friends decided to rag him... and oh, we did. Made the poor guy cry like hell."

Jenny fumed at Shekhar and the latter winked at her.

"We met as 'enemies' in school but destiny had some other plans. Exams were round the corner and I had to pass it to get to the 6th grade. It was easier earlier but too late did I realize that 5th grade was tougher than I thought and I had already received my fair share of thrashings from my parents. Not anymore, no way am I spending another year in 5th grade. My reputation was at stake.

Desperation kicked in and that is when I walked up to Karan, and asked his help. He was hesitant at first, it was natural for we didn't start off on good terms but that day, I guess for the first time in my life I pleaded for help. Karan was genuinely surprised and decided to help.

He had this habit of making notes. I know a lot of people do, nothing special really for it helps in the long run but I am talking about Karan here. At a very early age, he had this habit of creating plan A and Plan B. It was in our 11th grade I remember; he had named one of his plans as - DESPERATE MEASURES." Shekhar said.

Jenny burst out laughing. This was indeed a revelation for her.

"2 years into this relationship and you didn't notice that about him." Shekhar commented.

"I guess I am guilty of that but I don't know... he never really opened up about a lot of things. I once... asked him about his family. He became unusually silent. I thought... maybe I hurt him and apologized for it. He looked at me surprised, he smiled and said that I didn't have to. All I know his... he lost his father when he was but a baby. He doesn't remember anything about him." Jenny said looking concerned.

"Everyone has secrets. As long as those secrets are not an inconvenience to the others, it is best to keep them the way it is. You don't have to worry about Karan in that regard. I assure you. Coming back to my story, he gave me all his notes. I couldn't help but ask him as to why everything. What if I top scored in class? After all, Karan was one of the best students. Always in the top 5.

He smiled and said, 'I don't care about marks. There is no real metric to determine how knowledgeable someone is... that is only because every day, something new is happening and what we are learning today can become outdated in a matter of hours. I crave for knowledge and not marks. So, don't worry about me. Worry about yourself now. You need to pass.'

I could only stare at him. At that time, those words went over my head but today when I think about it, he never really cared about accolades, they just came to him because he did what he loved to do, whatever made him happy. All he ever wanted was peace of mind." Shekhar said.

"So how did he become the man who thrived on crisis?" Jenny asked.

"There was a basketball tournament. I was, and still good at it but my team was weak. Moreover, we needed a replacement just in case things went south. Back then, I didn't know that Karan was learning martial arts. His physique is a result of his dedication and discipline... you should know considering you are a martial artist too.

I approached him to be the replacement. I know he would refuse considering basketball is not his game but still I convinced him. He couldn't help laugh at the fact that I was a part of a weak team. He even asked me as to why I stuck up with them and not asked my sports master for a transfer. I couldn't ask. Call me naïve but... I loved my team even with all the limitations we had. Furthermore, I was the captain of the team. I couldn't desert them.

We were not even the underdogs considering our record of the no. of embarrassing defeats would make even the classic noobs say to themselves that we are better than them. I hold the record of being the high scorer but always in a losing cause. It was one of those days again where our opposition had already scored 12 goals and we were at 2. Karan was not playing but he sure was watching from the stands.

Karan couldn't believe what was going on. Suddenly, he wanted to do something to turn things around. During a brief timeout, he approached me and asked me as to what can be done to increase the score... win the match. I was clueless. I had no answer.

Karan then looked me in the eye and said – 'You are the top scorer so the burden is on you. I will round up the boys and our plan would be to pass the ball to you. Give me the word, the promise that you will score. Make every throw of yours count... and we will deal with the rest.'

I stared at him. I had to make the decision as fast as possible. I immediately had Karan join the team and lead the boys for me. Minutes, jenny... matter of minutes, Karan motivated the boys to not try anything stupid but to do just one thing. Grab the ball and pass it to me. Just snatch the ball from the opposition. It happened, Jenny. The boys did the same. We not only won the match... to this day, my score that day was an unbroken record which was beaten just a few months back by another student of my old school.

Karan is a different kind of leader, Jenny. He may not have a lot of skills but he has massive respect for people who are skilled. If he needs to get a work done... and if he can't do it, he won't think twice before asking the person who can do the work for him. What's more, he wouldn't shy away from telling his seniors that he got help from someone." Said Shekhar.

Jenny then remembered something, "Now that you are saying. Remember, we were on a mission on some remote island and we had to get through a door."

"Oh yes, the leader of that pack was hiding inside a safe house and the freaking terminal was just un-hackable. It changed passwords every 15 seconds and none of us were able to hack it." Shekhar also remembered.

"Karan was in a fix. He was frustrated though he did not show it. Suddenly, he remembered something and got in touch with the command center. The terminal had to be hacked not just to go inside the building but to increase the time it took to change passwords. A rep at the command center actually had the ability to do that and Karan immediately contacted him.

It worked. We got enough time on our hand to hack it. You did it and the door opened. I still remember the look on that leader's face when the door opened. He was quivering in fear, he did not even aim his gun at us which was fully loaded. He raised both his hands to signal that he surrendered." Said Jenny.

That was one hell of a mission. Still remember the class act with your sniper." Shekhar commented.

"Yeah, right. I wanted to tag along but Karan forced me to find a higher ground. Just because I am good with the sniper doesn't mean I am not good at close quarters." Jenny reacted.

"Whoa, easy girl! Maybe, my brother really loves you a lot, is possessive about you and wants to keep you safe. You gotta respect that!" Said Shekhar winking at Jenny again.

Jenny nodded in disagreement and said, "Oh really, by making me an easy target. The job of a sniper is riskier than ground support. Tell that to your 'possessive brother' who has not asked me for a cup of coffee for 15 days."

That very moment, Karan entered with a tray that had 4 cups of coffee on it and some donuts.

"Well, Jenny my love… and my Shekhar bro, I am really sorry about that." Karan said as he walked inside and placed the tray on the table.

Shekhar chuckled while Jenny and Karan looked at each other for a brief moment. Karan smiled and that was enough to make Jenny blush and look away for a moment.

"Where is Sulaiman?" Karan asked as he took a coffee and donut, and handed it over to Jenny.

"Must be in the hangar. He loves carriers and must be busy doing maintenance job even when it is not required." Shekhar said sinking his teeth on a hot and delicious donut.

Karan took a sip from his coffee cup and said, "We have a new mission. Tell him to come to our room on the double."

The door opened that time and Sulaiman came in.

"Speak of the devil." Jenny commented.

Karan and Shekhar chuckled while Sulaiman looked at them confused.

"What did I miss?" Sulaiman asked.

"You are just in time. Take a seat. We have a new mission." Karan answered.

"More bad guys to kill." Sulaiman said.

"On the contrary... though killing bad guys is always top priority for us... a few bad guys and a girl have emotionally and positively decided to become good guys. They want to help us destroy the Nationalist Corp." Karan responded.

"Destroy? Really?" Shekhar asked.

"This could be a trap. The anti-nationals are good at it. That is how they wiped out an entire squad who went on a reconnaissance mission. It all started with a beacon which was seemingly a BASE beacon reprogrammed by them to trap our guys." Said Jenny.

"And we were the same guys who tracked them down and made them pay for it." Said Karan.

"We are becoming 'popular' among those guys. Jenny could be right. Besides, rumors have spread of a mole in BASE but we are still unable to track the person." Said a concerned Sulaiman.

Karan nodded in agreement and said, "Agreed, but do we have a choice? As per the General, this could be a great opportunity to learn more about our enemy. We are talking about 3 people – Ajesh, Darshan and Shriya – who defected from the Nationalist Corp. They are seeking our help, they will provide all info and in return, they are requesting safety and..."

"And? And what?" Jenny asked.

"They want to join BASE as soldiers. They want to… you know… serve the nation and seek redemption for all the sins they have committed." Karan answered scratching his head in disbelief.

"I will blow their brains out before they 'seek redemption'. Sins, eh! I will make them sit and give them a 'discourse' of all the sins they committed and then put a bullet in their heads." Said a furious Shekhar.

"Calm down, Shekhar. I mean, guys, what if they want to help us? Only 2 things can happen – either it is a trap and no way in hell I am denying that or they really want to help us. It has been 4 years since that pyramid incident. Their activities are dwindling. We have really hit them hard yet I have a feeling something is off." Karan said.

"About what? What are you talking about?" Sulaiman asked.

"There are a lot of things which we know about the anti-nationals… yet there are certain things that seem off about them. We still have bits and pieces of info about them. We know they are a rogue army; they fight from the shadows most of the time. However, 4 years ago, they made a bold move and only because out of nowhere they got access to an ancient pyramid.

I mean what kind of army are we dealing with? They seem outdated from a distance, surprises us with something new, the same new surprise is straight out of the books of BASE which indicates a mole within us and then… out of nowhere they get their hands on a technology which normal humans can't comprehend.

The pyramid was destroyed. If we could have learned where they got access to it, this war would have been long over but no… we are back to square one." Karan explained.

"Any word on that mole? Are people still investigating it? We should have got some lead by this time!?" Jenny asked.

"No leads… or maybe, these people that we have been asked to extract, maybe they know about this mole. That is why this mission is important." Said Karan.

"Ok. As you say, Karan. We do want to get to the bottom of this. Go on, explain the mission." Said Shekhar.

Karan explained in detail, "The trio have defected from the anti-nationals. They have indicated that the army was born with an ideal that a lot of people accepted during its initial stages. However, few years into their war with BASE, something has changed. The leaders have become power hungry. People are fighting for top positions within the army.

They haven't revealed much due to the fact that they are been tracked and that is why they are seeking our help to extract them to a safe place so that they can reveal everything that they know.

They did say one thing – the anti-nationals are being led by an... you know... how to put this... entity."

The last sentence confused everyone with Sulaiman scratching his head.

"Karan, you ok? I mean... entity? What entity?" asked Shekhar.

"Like... an alien. Or something which cannot be classified as human. Is that what you are saying?" asked Jenny.

"This is a trap. They are throwing weird shit at us and we are buying it. Why? I agree with Shekhar. We should have triangulated their position then and there, and wiped them out without mercy." Sulaiman exclaimed.

"And that is why they are sending us. To wipe out any asshole throwing weird shit at us. So, Sulaiman, prep the carrier. We are going in. Let us get this over with." Karan said.

While closing his wrist monitor, Karan asked, "Any questions?"

The others raised their hands wanting to know more about the mission.

"Good. We will discuss them on the carrier. Now move out." Saying, Karan walked towards their designated armory.

The others nodded in disagreement and got up to prep themselves. After a few minutes, at the hangar, Sulaiman completed a last-minute check of their carrier with 2 other officers before the former gave a green light. Sulaiman got on to the pilot seat and powered up the engines while the rest strapped themselves on to their seats. Everyone prayed for a short while before Sulaiman flew the carrier out of the hangar and towards their target location.

After 10 minutes, Sulaiman made a confirmation, "Karan, we are close to the target. Should we contact them?"

"Yes, I will now. Keep flying to the target area and activate the friend and foe tracker. We should be wary of enemies lying in wait." Karan said and Sulaiman acknowledged.

The moment the tracker was switched on, Sulaiman found something odd.

"Karan, you might wanna see this." Said Sulaiman and Karan came towards the cockpit.

Karan could make out a series of dots moving at high speeds which indicated that either someone was chasing or was being chased. Suddenly, there was a distress signal and someone was trying to contact them.

"Ajesh to BASE command, please respond. We are under heavy fire. Seeking assistance. Please respond. Please respond. Over."

"Ajesh! He is one of them, right? The one we need to extract." Sulaiman said.

Karan immediately got on the radio, "Ajesh. This is Major Bose. We hear you. What is going on down there?"

"Major Bose. They found us and are tailing us. We need your help." Ajesh replied.

They could hear gunfire through the radio.

"This was not what I expected." Said Karan.

"We need to help them but they are in the city. We cannot go guns blazing. Civilians will get caught in the fire." Said Sulaiman.

"Guys, we got a problem." Shekhar alerted everyone and at that very moment, the alarms on the carrier started to ring.

"Storm warning!? Are you serious!?" Sulaiman was alarmed at this development.

Karan looked at the screen which indicated the location of the storm. He then rushed back to look at it. It was not a common storm.

"Guys, double armor. Immediately. It is an acid rain storm." Karan alerted everyone and others yielded bringing out their protective gear.

"Major, what is going on? We need assistance. Our vehicle cannot stand more of this assault." Ajesh said.

"We got another problem, Ajesh. It is an acid rain storm. You need to get out of the city." Karan responded.

"Say what!?" Ajesh reacted.

"What happened? What are they saying?" Darshan asked.

"An acid rain storm. It is coming right at us." Ajesh communicated the information.

At that very moment, the group could hear sirens wailing. People got to know its purpose and panicked. The group could see a few people closing their shops while the rest running away towards their home.

"We chose the wrong day to defect." Darshan commented.

Firing had stopped for a moment considering both the trio and nationalist corp soldiers were wondering what to do next.

Back at the carrier, Sulaiman noticed something.

"Karan, about 2 clicks north west, there is a chemical factory. It is abandoned as per the map." Sulaiman informed.

"Abandoned factory, eh! Any information about its condition?" Karan asked.

"Not much but if we have to survive that storm, we need a place to hide and wait." Sulaiman answered.

"Right then. Head to that factory. Send the location of the same to Ajesh. I will inform him." Said Karan.

Karan took out his protective gear and simultaneously got on his radio, "Ajesh, none of us are going anywhere. Not until the storm passes. We have sent the location of an abandoned chemical factory. Head over there and we will meet up."

"Tch! Alright, we are headed there." Said Ajesh.

The location was received and Ajesh passed it over to Darshan, saying, "Head over here. We need to survive first before we think of anything."

Darshan nodded in agreement and stepped on the gas.

The trident squad had reached the city and Sulaiman boosted the carrier engines to reach the factory faster. He noticed the trio in the car driving towards the designated location but they were not the only one.

"Safe to say they got the message but we have uninvited guests too." Sulaiman informed.

"No time to entertain them. Send them back... with a bang." Karan ordered and Sulaiman acknowledged.

2 missiles perfectly aimed in between the vehicles and the 3 anti-national SUVs were destroyed.

"Look at them fly!" Sulaiman reacted.

The acid rain storm was close now. Sulaiman spotted a landing pad.

"The carrier will take a beating if we keep it outside on the landing pad. We have no idea how long the storm will continue." Said Sulaiman.

"The landing pad should have a lift system. It can take us down and then we can close the hatch. We need to stick inside the carrier till it is done." Jenny said.

"It is abandoned. We need to get the lights running. The shield system should hold out long but we will have to get the power running or we will be trapped here." Shekhar suggested.

"The anti-nationals know they defected. They will send in troops. We have protective cover but we cannot underestimate the enemy after what we have been dealing with for years. Fighting will still be difficult in this condition." Said Karan.

"Test of survival, buddy. We need to keep everything in check so that when the skies clear, we can bow out ASAP." Shekhar stated.

While the trio had reached the factory and got in safely, Sulaiman landed the carrier on to the landing pad. It started raining and the protective suit meter indicated unsafe situation outside.

"Suit is green so we can walk but we cannot remain outside for long." said Jenny.

The team got out. Shekhar spotted the landing pad switch, he jogged towards it and clicked it but it did not work.

"We have work cut out for us." Shekhar commented.

"No argument on that. Shekhar, Sulaiman... see if you can get the power back. Jenny, let us meet the trio. They will need the protective suit too." Said Karan.

Everyone acknowledged and they walked down with Karan and Jenny carrying protective gear cases with them. The trio had sat down on some boxes keeping their distances from areas where the acidic water was dripping or sprinkling from.

CHAPTER TWO

FROM UNKNOWN TO KNOWN

"This factory has seen better days but by the looks of it at present... not for long. Wear these gears to stay protected. We have a fight in our hands but the storm has given us time to prepare." Karan said.

The trio took the gears and wore them.

"Change of plans from what I can see. You people were supposed to be interrogated in BASE but we will have to do it over here. If you guys have no issues with it." Karan stated.

Ajesh looked at his friends who nodded in agreement. They had much to talk and they knew BASE needed to know everything. They were the trump cards for stopping an ongoing war.

"We are eager to speak, Major. If this how it has to be, then we are game for it." Ajesh responded.

"Then we are good." Said Karan.

Jenny had set up the communication device but there was a problem.

"Signal strength is weak due to the storm. We cannot broadcast the interrogation to BASE command. I can boost the signal but only if I have access to a communication tower or terminal." Said Jenny.

"This factory should have a terminal but not sure if it will work." Said Karan.

That moment, there was a loud buzz sound which indicated that the power was back.

"They did it." Jenny reacted.

Shekhar and Sulaiman joined the group. While Sulaiman walked towards his teammates, Shekhar looked at the trio. He slowly walked towards them and looked into Ajesh's eyes.

"Karan, I don't like the look of this." Sulaiman commented.

"Just wait and watch. This should be interesting." Said Karan with a smirk.

Shekhar kept staring at Ajesh and the latter started to feel uncomfortable. Shekhar then backed off and stared at the others. He then started sniffing them like a dog.

"Karan, stop him. This is gross." Jenny said tugging at Karan.

"He is just playing with them. Besides, they want to be a part of BASE, right? Let us assume they are a part of it and therefore, give them a 'proper' welcome. Remember how we were welcomed." Karan said.

"Don't know about you guys but we ladies had a real 'welcome' from some real 'gentlemen' who were trying to prove they were alpha males or something." Jenny commented.

Karan and Sulaiman looked at each other with a wicked smile.

Shekhar suddenly aimed his rifle at them. The trio were taken aback, they pulled out their firearm and aimed at the former. The standoff was brief though as Shekhar put his rifle down and walked towards his teammates laughing heartily while the trio looked at each other confused.

"You had your fun? We have work to do." Karan asked.

"I thought we are working. What is the hold up?" Shekhar asked as he glanced at the communication device.

"Well done with the power but we need to do something about the comm channels. Signal is weak. We need to amplify it to allow broadcasting." Jenny explained.

"Do you now? Well, the terminal you are looking for is outside. With the storm outside, we cannot go there at the moment. We should have been in BASE now interrogating them." Shekhar responded.

"Well, let us hope the storm passes soon enough. We will have to record this. Whatever we record is important and we cannot lose that data. Not at any cost. Set up the camera, Jenny. Let us start. Shekhar and Sulaiman, activate the tracker. Keep watch and alert immediately if we get company.

Our enemies are not sitting around. They will find a way. Our experience has taught us one thing. They always find a way... and that is alarming to say the least." Saying, Karan walked towards the trio.

"What was that all about?" Ajesh asked.

"Oh that... WELCOME TO BASE!" Karan answered and the trio stared at the latter shocked.

The camera was set up and with jenny giving the signal that recording had begun, the interrogation began too.

"Not my first interrogation but definitely the easiest one considering the 'customer' in front is ready to talk. Unlike the others who act that they are tough but after a few minutes, start crying like a baby." Karan commented.

"I did cry like a baby and that was just once. It was also that moment that made me take this drastic step." Ajesh stated and Karan raised his eyebrows in wonder.

"So... what happened? And why do you want to side with us?" Karan asked.

Ajesh took a deep breath and looked outside. The storm still persisted and so did the storm inside him. He started, "Major, I am going to reveal everything. It does not matter whether you know it or do not know it. What matters is the knowledge of who or what you are dealing with... and what is about to come. You are free to interrupt me with questions which I will gladly answer, however, I would expect that you hear us out without any prejudice.

The Nationalist Corp (TNC)... Anti-Nationals, in your vocabulary.... has been in existence for over 30 years. We as foot soldiers are not aware of its founding members. We... do not have that authority but what we do know is that it is, by all means, a rogue regime that was started to go against BASE.

The autonomy of that organization was declared evil by the founders and therefore, they sought to recruit people who were against the evil. Lo and behold, it did get followers. Some who disbelieved autonomy, some who were not happy with their lives being governed by the military and many who faced trouble in the hands of the soldiers of BASE."

"So which category you are in?" Sulaiman asked with a concerned look that impressed Ajesh.

"I was 21 when my mom died due to a road accident. I had just got a job but it was not enough to pay for hospital bills. Insurance was the last resort but I did not get it. You want to know why? BASE has certain officers who help in regards to insurance claims by checking if the victim really deserves it or not.

I got to know that it was my mom's fault. She was trying to cross the road when the signal was green and in doing so, got run over. We did not get the insurance. I was angry but anger cannot save my mom. I somehow managed to get the money but it was too late. She was long gone." Ajesh said, tears rolled down his eyes.

"And that was your motivation to join the anti-nationals?" Asked Shekhar.

"No, but I was contacted by an anti-national who 'motivated' me to take arms against BASE. That is how my journey with the TNC began. I was young, angry... and there was no one to guide me. No one to tell me the right from wrong." Ajesh answered.

Shekhar was not convinced. He wanted to say something but then remained silent looking away from everyone.

"And the others? Shriya? Darshan?" Jenny asked.

Shriya and Darshan looked at each other. They hesitated but they knew they were answerable. They have committed crimes but the question was the severity of their crimes.

"Shriya is my sister. It was 12 years ago, my sister... was gangraped and thrown to the streets. She was saved by some locals who rushed her to the hospital. We were not so well off and were working day in and day out trying to make ends meet.

I worked in a factory while she was working in a bar. Initially, I thought that it was a bunch of hooligans who had targeted her. I was in rage. I wanted to kill them. I did actually. I was able to track down 2 of them and in a fit of rage killed them.

And then, I saw the badge... BASE... I was shocked. I could have escaped from there but I stood there shocked. Soldiers of BASE, they raped my sister. By the time I could decide what to do, crowds had gathered and along with them, BASE soldiers who apprehended me.

I don't know what happened after that. All I remember is that I was released through a back door and was introduced to a man who had a strong hatred for BASE. He fed on my anger and my will for vengeance, and asked me to join a regime which was in war with BASE. That is how we joined the TNC."

Shekhar who was already suspicious about the trio couldn't contain himself. He threw his gun, walked towards Darshan and caught him by his collar.

"You think you can spit bullshit about our corp and get away with it, you swine." Saying, Shekhar started punching him.

The others including Ajesh tried to pull Shekhar and Darshan from each other. While Ajesh pulled Darshan away, Karan and his squad tried to contain Shekhar.

"Stop it, Shekhar. For God's sake, control yourself." Jenny shouted.

"I am not going to believe them. Even if you order me to do it, Karan, I am not going to. Those Anti-national bastards can go to hell for all I care." Shekhar retorted.

"Shekhar, calm down and listen to me. LISTEN TO ME." Karan caught hold of Shekhar's collar now and looked into his eyes feigning anger.

Shekhar looked at Karan. The former was still angry but he was listening.

"You heard them. Isn't it? You heard every word they spoke. Am I the only one who understands or realizes that these people were approached by someone who may or may not be the mole that BASE is trying to look for all these years?" Karan asked.

Shekhar stared at Karan and so did the others. Karan let of Shekhar's collar, the latter continued to stare at Karan, he then looked at the trio. He stayed silent and looked away from everyone. Karan was not sure if he was feeling ashamed for his action or he was still angry but the interrogation was top priority. He walked back but not before glancing towards Shekhar who banged his fist against a pipe.

"I am sorry for what happened. Please sit down. I assure you. It won't happen again." Said Karan.

Anti-nationals or not, they were still their guest and Karan did feel ashamed about what happened.

"Major. Don't feel bad. This was expected. We have nothing against Lt. Shekhar but when we are being interrogated, it is our duty to reveal everything and not hide any secrets.

Yes, these are our reason for joining TNC but things have changed. We are at fault for not realizing in time that we were on the path of doom. I don't know whether we are too late or not in realizing that we have committed a sin and maybe... maybe, we will never get a chance or no one will give us the chance to redeem ourselves.

As long as fate has kept us alive, we will not stay silent. We will reveal everything and, in that way, hope that Lt. Shekhar in due course will understand that we, the 3 of us, are no more the enemy." Said Ajesh.

Karan smiled and nodded in agreement, also indicating the trio to sit down.

"So, Darshan, you stated you were able to track down 2 of them and kill them but what about the others? Any idea?" Karan asked.

"Not really. Besides, it has years since that incident. Whoever it was who wanted me and my sister to join the regime just wanted to fuel my taste for revenge. Of course, initially there was no action when we joined.

The nationalist corp follow the same hierarchy as any organization would. Don't be surprised if what I say it is similar to what BASE follows but let me assure you, it is not so formal as it looks. Informal, no way in hell! We were at ground level and treated as cannon fodder. We were assigned to do odd jobs for the corp while there were others who joined before us who were assigned dangerous tasks.

The nationalist corp was running on stolen or borrowed tech. Half of the people even in higher post did not understand how to use it. Worst, they were hardly concerned and expected us to memorize procedures to handle those techs." Darshan said.

"This is ridiculous. We have fought with you people and seen you use our own stuff against us. Now you are saying that so long we were fighting with people who had no idea what they were brandishing." Karan reacted visibly alarmed.

"I still remember a moment when a sniper almost grazed my head when we were on a mission. I still have nightmares about it and you are saying that you people are bunch of illiterates. Stop playing us." Sulaiman spoke up.

"We are not, Sir. This is the reality. There are exceptions like Ajesh over here who is a crack shot with the sniper. Not sure if he was the one who fired at you but we have our share of fighting with BASE soldiers. We have... killed... a lot of them but only because of lies fed to us. All anti-nationalist soldiers are mostly survivors out for revenge but there are those who have hatred for BASE. People who are against anything that has the word BASE carved on it." said Darshan.

"But who was funding this regime? How were you people paid? How were you surviving?" Karan asked.

"No idea. Trust me, Major. We can tell you who is directing the flop show but we have no idea of the fool producing or financing it. As Darshan said, we were cannon fodder. Soldiers were just selected randomly to go to designated targets. It could be anything. Stealing rations, attacking a weapons depot, killing or attacking a group or squad of BASE soldiers... weird as it sounds, we didn't realize it until 5 years back." Said Ajesh.

"What was it? What happened 5 years back?" Karan asked.

Ajesh became morose but shriya nudged him to continue.

"We were 20 of us who were selected to raid a depot for supplies. We did raid it but there were casualties. We were able to get away with a few but in that effort, we lost 15 soldiers. One of us, my best friend, Yousuf, was gravely injured.

Major, what would you do if one of your team mates is injured? What would you do... if you knew in your heart that you cannot save your friend? You will still try, isn't it? That is what I did. I thought it was my duty.

We all escaped from there and reached the meeting point. My senior officer looked at the supplies. He wasn't happy about it and it was obvious. He then looked at my friend who was in bad shape and needed medical attention. I pleaded for it but my officer.... He pulled out his sidearm and put a bullet in his head." Tears welled up as Ajesh said that.

Karan and his team were genuinely shocked. They looked at each other trying to understand this brutality.

"Why? Why did he kill him?" Jenny asked.

Ajesh answered, "I asked. I did ask and I asked in anger. He pointed the sidearm at me. He could have pulled the trigger but he didn't. It was understood that I was the best. I could have climbed up the ranks. In due course been in his shoes. He knew it so he warned me. He said – We are not running a charity here. You see the supplies you got. These supplies will run only for month and a half and not more than that. We have a lot of mouths to feed. Death is a blessing in this regime, Ajesh. His food and his supplies can be utilized by someone who is alive.

We need men and women to spread our beliefs, ideas and thoughts but we lack funds. Food, water, supplies, money... we lack all of it. Where are we going to find it? You think we have a treasure house with never ending money. As long as you people are alive, you are useful to this regime. Get injured or get captured, we are no use to the regime.

Kill with brutal intent or die in honor but never ever get captured or injured. That is how this regime will live and thrive."

There was silence. No one spoke a word for a minute.

"Now I get it. Now I see why we have never been able to capture an anti-national alive. Why they always kill themselves before being captured and while committing suicide, end up killing our soldiers too. Every single anti-national is a suicide bomber. And that is why, we have no choice but to finish them off.

This is... perhaps... the first time ever that we are interrogating them and that is only because they... they have agreed to come forward and reveal the truth. The regime knows about this. They are looking for an opportunity to finish them off before their secrets are revealed." Jenny explained.

Karan and Sulaiman looked at each other and nodded in agreement. Shekhar was still silent trying to digest what Darshan said before. He then noticed a storehouse adjacent to the floor they were in and decided to investigate it.

CHAPTER THREE

COMMS UP

"Remember Code Red?" Ajesh asked.

"Yes, that coward. The only thing I remember about him is that he was always the first to scurry while leaving his men to do his job. Moreover, he wore a mask." Karan replied.

Ajesh smirked and said, "Not sure if he is a coward but yes, that weird mask of his. He has more haters than admirers. He is hero to a few people, rose among the ranks as quickly as others, killed a lot of BASE soldiers and was hunted for the same.

He has or had a squad of his own. Navin, a friend of mine was a member of that squad. The last thing I know, he was there along with Code Red on that pyramid. I take it he died while Code Red... as usual... escaped."

"He is probably dead. We killed his squad while trying to stop the pyramid from exploding. If he was one of them, we.... we definitely killed him." Sulaiman answered.

"No, I don't think so." Karan said and the others stared at him surprised.

Karan explained, "Strange that you people did not notice. The place where the timer was had 5 people guarding it. However, while we realized that we couldn't stop the timer and instead were waiting to die, I noticed the dead body of an anti-national lying one floor beneath us.

I know it was... you know, an emotional moment for us but I remember seeing that dead body. We managed to escape in time. It has been 4 years since then. I know I never revealed this to anyone but my mind kept going back to that dead body. Something happened over there before we reached that area.

Now that you spoke about your friend, about Code Red's squad... I suddenly remembered that dead body. How did it reach there? What happened over there?"

"Why do I have the feeling that it has to be Navin? Navin hated him yet he couldn't stand up against him. Code Red is ruthless, he doesn't listen to anyone and his concept of leadership is very simple – Do as you are told or die.

He doesn't care for his people, his squad... nobody. Yet he is a favorite among the higher ranks and he enjoys being their lap dog. A lot of people have died under him. People shiver in fear to be named as one of his squad mates because they feel that it is the fastest way to heaven... or hell." Ajesh said.

At that moment, Shekhar stepped in to give the good news.

"There is a way to get into the communication tower. We do not have to go outside and risk our lives." Shekhar said holding a map.

"Well, well! Someone was busy with treasure hunting." Sulaiman commented.

"We are all ears, Shekhar. What have you got?" Karan asked.

"A problem. There is a way but it is through the sewers." Shekhar responded.

"That... can be handled. We have all been through enough 'shit' in our life to face any challenge the sewers will offer." Said Sulaiman.

"No arguments on that. I don't see any reason why you should call it a problem." Jenny said.

"Do you know the reason why this factory was closed?" Shekhar asked.

The people looked at each other.

"Ruts." Shriya answered, and everyone turned towards her.

"Exactly. She is intelligent. Learn a thing or two from her, Jenny." Shekhar commented.

The trio looked at each other confused while Karan and Sulaiman looked at each other and smiled. Shekhar was back in his element. Jenny was happy too and therefore, did not shy away from engaging in a banter.

"Yeah, right! Remind me that we are in a beauty pageant." Jenny said.

"You will still lose. Now, shut up and listen." Said Shekhar.

This was enough to brighten up everyone including the trio. The tense atmosphere disappeared suddenly even with the storm still raging outside. Shekhar had brought a container with him to act as a table, signaling Jenny to come closer. She sat in between Karan and Sulaiman. Placing the map over the container so that everyone can see, he continued, "This is the communication tower. Not sure if it is in working condition but I guess we will sort it out. We need to pass through the sewers which is more a maze then a simple ramp walk. The map is handy so it should be easy to find the location of the doorway that will lead to the tower.

Now, the rut problem. It is obvious we couldn't call pest control to eradicate them so BASE was called in. A mission was organized which led to a lot of casualties. It is said that close to 250 soldiers were killed in an attempt to eradicate them."

The people were shocked to hear this.

"I don't understand. Why are we not aware of such an incident? And how do you people know about these creatures?" Sulaiman asked.

"Well, I did hear about them but still not much is spoken about it. It is somewhat of a classified encounter whose results have been kept under wraps." Jenny stated.

"Exactly. What I am revealing now is just plain rumor. I have never encountered them but I have heard of them." Shekhar said.

"But we have encountered them. Seen them with our own eye." Darshan said and everyone's attention turn towards him.

Darshan continued, "Ajesh was not on this mission but shriya and I were. Incidentally, we witnessed the massacre of your soldiers. Saw it with our own eyes and before we know, we were also embroiled. We lost our own people but Shriya, I and a few others managed to survive and live to tell the tale.

Not sure why it was classified by BASE, Ms. Jenny but trust us, it is true and even today, we have nightmares regarding it. It was 3 years ago, about 6 squads were sent in to this factory to raid it and also take hostages. The motive was simple, to threaten BASE to fulfil our demands but we were in for a surprise. Something which even the Nationalist Corp leaders never saw it coming.

The plan was to enter through the sewers. A map was arranged for the same. It would have been a surprise attack but never did we realize that we were to be surprised. We did enter the sewers; it is more of a labyrinth and we had to stick to the route properly marked on the map. We were close to reaching the factory when we heard voices.

We were shocked to see BASE soldiers. What were they doing over there? What was their job over there? We hid ourselves and from a distance tried to understand what was going on. They were setting up turrets and then splitting up in search of something... but what? Suddenly, I looked right and my eyes fell on something... something huge and hideous slowly coming towards one of our squads.

Before I could alert anyone, more started to appear and they pounced on our squad. We watched in horror as the creatures mercilessly tore apart those poor souls. Their screams still give me nightmares. BASE soldiers were alerted by it and they rushed towards the area. Firing began and more of those hideous creatures started to appear.

They were tall, at least 6-7 feet in height. They were agile and could leap at great heights. They were giant rats, yes but their build was exactly like we humans. You can call them humanoids. As firing was going on, we decided to escape from there but we lost the maps in that turmoil.

We were on our own but we had no choice. We ran from that area with the hope that we will find a way. We were 35 of us. I guess the almighty was with us as we found our escape route. Only 7 of us survived. It was all over the news and we reported everything to the leadership."

All were wonder struck listening to this.

"What was BASE's account about this incident?" Jenny asked.

"200 soldiers lost their lives in that incident but unlike the anti-nationals, we had the tech support to deal with this. Heavy weapons and mechs were used, Dr. Prakash who was working on a chemical weapon decided to utilize this mission to test it and it worked.

The population of those rodents diminished and a final report was brought out stating that the danger had passed. However, due to heavy use of the chemical weapon, this place was rendered uninhabitable and therefore, the factory was closed. The owners received compensation for the damages and heavy loss.

There has been no further news about the Ruts. It has been 3 years and there have been no sightings too." Karan responded.

"How do you know all this?" Sulaiman asked.

"I heard only a gist of it from someone. I got curious and wanted to know more. I realized that it was confidential but I still had access to such accounts. Yet some of it was blacked out, which is obvious but what I said just now was mentioned on that file." Karan replied.

"I take it that it was a black day for both sides. Now, this chemical bomb that... you were talking about. How much was used and is it still active after 3 years?" Ajesh asked.

"Good question. If we have to make it to the comm tower, we need to pass through the sewer with all that gas." Sulaiman added.

"We have gas masks so shouldn't be a problem. As for the rodent problem, I hope we don't run into any." Karan responded.

"And what if? How should we deal with them? There are no photos or videos that we can look at to 'motivate' ourselves. All we have is Darshan's account... and that is scary enough." Shekhar commented.

"Do we have a choice? The storm is not going to last long. Once it passes, we have the anti-nationals to deal with and they are going to throw everything at us to get rid of these three. They have only revealed maybe 10% of their dirty little secrets but there is more.

We need time and a powerful comm system to document and transmit the interrogation to BASE command. At present, sorry for saying this, their words carry more value than our lives and that is the intent we all need to keep. Unless, you people have a better option." Karan said.

The others looked at each other and thought hard.

"Karan is right. We need to take a chance. If escape is not an option when the enemy is upon us, at least their words need to reach BASE command. Transmitting won't take time, I assure you but if we fail, we fail at gathering information that can help us win the war." Jenny added.

"Well then, it is decided. We are going. Better be armed enough before we head out." Shekhar said.

"Right you are. Let us head back to the carrier first and re-check our weapons. Moreover, these 3 also need to be armed and ready to face whatever is beyond that door. Looks like we don't have to test you separately when it comes to joining BASE. This mission here is the perfect test.

This is no longer just our mission. From here on, it is your mission too. We are all in this together. We have to look out for each other if we have to survive this. Any questions, now is the time." Karan said.

Ajesh, Shriya and Darshan looked at each other and smiled, looking back at Karan, they replied, "No questions."

The soldiers checked their weaponry and stocked up on ammunitions. The trio chose their weapons albeit guidance from Sulaiman. Some heavy weapons were also taken. Once the soldiers were satisfied with their stock, they headed towards the door.

Before opening the door, Karan spoke again, "We may not come back through this door again but if things go south, nothing should come out of this door. We need to make sure whatever threat is in there, it remains there. Understood?"

The others nodded in agreement after which Karan slowly opened the hatch. The others readied their weapons waiting for anything to pounce on them if the door opens. Karan took a deep breath and pushed the door open. The soldiers waited for a minute for anything to appear. It was dark so they switched on the lights. They also activated the night vision mode to detect any movement.

"Nothing in sight. Should we move in?" Shekhar asked.

"Yes, keep the lights on and the mode on. Stick together, stay alert... and yell, I repeat, yell if you see any movement." said Karan as he led on.

CHAPTER FOUR

HORROR TECH

Shekhar led the way, continuously looking at the map to avoid going in circles while the others looked around, weapons ready.

"Why do I have the feeling that someone or something is looking at us?" Jenny asked.

"If it comforts you, Mam... even I have the same feeling." said Ajesh.

"We are in this together, Ajesh. How about you call me by name." Jenny stated which surprised the trio.

Karan added, "She is right. It was our duty to bring you to BASE safely but we are in a situation where we have to look out for each other. You free to call us by our names... if you are comfortable with it."

The trio looked at each other and agreed.

"Alright... Karan... and Jenny. As you wish but what about your friend who is leading us?" Asked Shriya.

"I hate people calling me, sir... and I also have a good mind to kill you all if things go south. So, decide what you want to call me." Shekhar answered.

His squad chuckled at the answer while Karan looked at the trio.

"Your friend, Shekhar, sure is full of contradictions. I will take my chance if the need arises." Ajesh answered.

The group reached an area which led to multiple paths.

"Alright, 4 paths but one of them leads to the door to the communication tower. And that path, Ladies and Gentlemen, is the 3rd one. Let's move." Shekhar said.

"Shh, guys, I hear something. Right side." Darshan alerted everyone and the others aimed their gun at the same direction.

The group could hear a scratching sound followed by squeaks.

"Those rodents growl... or squeak?" Shriya asked.

Sulaiman signaled Darshan to set the turrets and activate auto mode. Darshan did the same but both soldiers were confused when it wasn't signaling anything and lay dormant.

That very moment, 5 rats came out and was sniffing the air.

The people couldn't believe this but couldn't help feeling a sigh of relief.

"Irony! Let's move before a big surprise appears." Said Karan.

Suddenly, the turrets started to fire alarming the group. Sulaiman was quick to realize that the turrets were trying to lock on to a target or targets.

"Everyone, get down. Quick... or we will be caught in the line of fire." Sulaiman said and the others heeded.

The turrets were firing continuously but was having a hard time getting a lock on. Soon, 4-5 giant ruts came out of their hiding. The group stared at them in shock and awe, they were 7 feet tall and walked on 2 legs. At first glance, they looked like wolves but one look at their face made it clear as day that they were oversized rats that turned humanoids, but how?

"We are dead meat if we stay here. We have to break for the door. Take our chance." Shekhar yelled.

Karan replied, "On my signal, everyone goes through the 3rd door. Stay close or we will end up leaving anyone or all behind."

More ruts were dropping in while 3 were down due to the turret fire. Karan gave the signal and the group dashed through the 3rd door.

"Run. Run. Don't wait for anything or anyone. The first to reach the door... get it open. Just get that damn thing open." Karan yelled.

Ajesh and Sulaiman were the first to reach. Sulaiman yanked at the handle which had jammed due to age, a strong hit from the butt of his rifle and the handle came down. Ajesh did not waste time as he opened the door and yelled at the others to run inside.

When the others reached the door, Shriya was the first to notice that the firing had stopped. Soon, it dawned on everyone.

"Darshan? Darshan, where are you?" Shriya shouted.

Karan also noticed another one missing.

"Where is Jenny?" Karan asked with a concerned tone.

Shekhar did an immediate head count. 2 people were missing.

"We have to save them. We can leave them behind." Said Shriya, she was starting to panic as she walked towards Ajesh.

Shekhar and Sulaiman looked at Karan who was still looking at the way they were all running in from. They came forward to trying to listen intently for the sound of footsteps but there was none.

"Karan, she is... she is gone. They both... They..." Shekhar spoke up but Karan took a deep breath and proactively pulled out his squad tracker.

"She is... she is alive. Look, her blink... it is..." As Karan was speaking, everyone came closer and looked at it.

Not just her blink but another blink could be detected. Shekhar was quick to notice that it was the 2nd pathway.

"We have to help them. We have to help them. We cannot leave them behind." Shriya said.

Karan was still looking at the tracker, Shekhar could make out that the former was having a hard time making a decision. Still, he was their leader and he had to make one.

"Karan, we are all in this together. Say the word and we will go by it." Shekhar said trying to calm Karan down.

Karan looked at Shekhar, he was breathing heavily. He looked away and closed his eyes for a moment. Then taking a deep breath, he asked, "Shekhar, where does the 2nd path lead to? What does the map say?"

Shekhar looked at the map. It didn't state anything, he looked at Karan and nodded indicating he had no idea.

"I have a feeling they took the wrong path. We need to get them back. Not sure why the firing stopped but we need to find out." Karan said.

"I though the ruts were annihilated. Where did they come from?" Sulaiman asked.

"Safe to say they aren't. We need to find where they came from but first, we need to see where did Jenny and Darshan go." Ajesh responded.

"Their blinks... have disappeared. I don't see them... in the tracker." Karan said.

Indeed, the trackers had gone dark. There was nothing. Karan took a deep breath again, he looked at the door that led to the communication tower and then back at the way they came from. He took a grip of himself and made up his mind.

"We are going back. The sudden appearance of the ruts is disturbing. We need to find the source. I have a feeling the rut threats have not passed. BASE needs to know this but only after we have confirmed evidence." Karan said.

The others agreed. They backtracked to the ambush point and cautiously moved around in pairs to check for trouble.

"No use wasting time. Move into the 2nd path and be wary of your surroundings." Said Karan and the other acknowledged.

As they walked through the 2nd path, Ajesh noticed something.

"Guys, we are been watched. I don't know what or who but we are." Ajesh informed.

Sure enough, everyone spotted a camera and slowly, the people were able to see more cameras.

"Who is watching us? The ruts? Are they... so advanced?" asked Shekhar.

"Whoa, Guys, come on! Seriously! You are forgetting where we are, is it? This was a factory, remember?" Sulaiman asked sarcastically.

The group looked at each other still wondering.

"The factory dealt with toxic materials. These materials were shown as the reason for the ruts appearing. Are we... moving into a mine?" Karan asked.

"Let us keep moving. We don't want that person... or entity to wait for us. Our host, whoever, it is... is already angry that we trespassed. Let us not make 'it' angrier." Said Shekhar.

The group continued on till they reached a door similar to the one in the 3rd path.

"Behind Door No. 3... was our freedom. Behind Door no. 2...!?" Ajesh spoke up.

"We are in for a surprise. The issue is... we may not like it." Sulaiman responded.

The group was then jolted by a loud sound and were shocked to see the door open by itself.

"Our host does like to receive guests but that doesn't mean the person will not be a hostile. Stay together, people. Hate to tell you but we are walking into a trap." Karan said.

The group walked in to see stairs leading downwards. It was dark so the group switched on their flashlights. It wasn't required as the mysterious entity had switched the lights of the stairs making it easier to watch everything in the distance.

"Karan, Karan, can you hear me? Please respond." The people heard a voice on their comms.

"Jenny. Jenny, is that you?" Karan replied, his voice echoed down the stairway.

"Shhh, quiet. Keep your voice down. They might hear you. I am sending you the coordinates of my location. Come and meet me there. You need to see this." Jenny replied.

"Darshan, is he alright? Is he with you?" Shriya asked with a concerned tone.

There was no answer. Shriya looked at Ajesh, she was starting to panic again for not receiving a reply.

"Shriya, the reason I took the 2nd path was because I saw Darshan being dragged by a rut. I couldn't leave him behind. While the other ruts were killed, one of them survived and dragged Darshan away. I ran behind it but it was too fast.

Luckily, the door you people came through was open long enough for me to get in. It locked out behind me and there was no way to go back. I found a comm center here after some exploring and that is where I am speaking from.

I will explain everything but you guys need to reach me. A big secret was hiding right below us and no one caught a wind of it." Jenny answered.

Shriya was in tears now but Ajesh tried to console her.

"Don't worry. We will get him back. He will be fine." Ajesh said.

"Yes, we will. We are the ones who were tasked to get you people to BASE safely and we will do just that. Don't worry, Shriya. Jenny, coordinates received and confirmed. We are heading there." Karan said.

As they walked towards the comm center, Shekhar whispered to Karan, "Big secret, eh! Did Jenny find some treasure?"

"For all I know, this 'treasure' sure is toxic in nature. Let us hurry. It looks like we can utilize that comm center to broadcast our data... or at least call for help." Karan replied.

As the group reached the location, they stopped in their path and gasped in horror.

"Yes, I had the same expression." Jenny commented.

The group were in a large room with huge glass tanks and in those tanks were ruts. It was not clear whether they were hibernating or kept unconscious but the group could see monitors attached to the tanks that were showing pulse rates.

"They... are... alive. Asleep. Like... I don't understand." Shriya spoke up trying to keep a distance from the tanks.

Karan had a look at one of the monitors attached to a tank.

"Stable but how? How are they kept in a stable condition?" Karan asked.

"There is someone out there who is running the show here. We need to find the handler." Said Shekhar.

Karan spotted Jenny in the control room; the latter waved at him. The group took the stairs and Jenny opened the doors. As the group came in, Karan and Jenny hugged each other while the others looked on.

"I am ok, Karan. Don't worry." Jenny comforted Karan.

Karan didn't say anything. He kept silent and smiled indicating that he was relieved.

"You people need to see something. This is not the only room. There is something else." Jenny said as she walked towards a console.

"This place is deserted. Did you see anyone, Jenny or it was like this when you discovered it?" Ajesh asked.

"Yes, it was like this. Mysterious considering everything over here is in automation. Systems are working around the clock. The factory above is abandoned but not this place." Jenny replied.

"But where is the power coming from? Where is the source?" Shekhar asked.

"That is what I am going to show you." Jenny said as she typed something on the keyboard and then signaled everyone to look at the screen.

The group were astounded.

"Is that a dam?" Shriya asked.

"To be specific. It is a hydroelectric dam. Water flowing underground is being used to run this facility. Whoever built it is a genius, no doubt." Jenny replied.

"Agreed but what is the reason for it? Why is so much power required?" Karan asked.

"Oh yes, I have the answer to that too." Saying, Jenny clicked a keyboard button which changed cameras.

The group came closer to see a giant tank but it was not a glass tank. The room was obviously larger than the room they were in. The group could make out high amount of power being diverted towards the same room.

"What is in it?" Ajesh asked.

"Look at the size of it. Don't tell it houses something... you know, something bigger than a Rut." Shekhar commented.

"Care to take a look. We came this far so better explore a bit..." Karan started but stopped.

"Karan, what happened?" Sulaiman asked.

Karan was looking at the screen and everyone did the same. They gasped as they saw 2 ruts dragging Darshan. They stopped right in front of the giant tank. A few seconds later, an old man wearing a strange uniform came closer and had a look at Darshan. He was saying something.

"Can you activate the audio?" Karan asked.

Jenny tried but by the time it could be activated, the group saw Darshan been taken away and all they could hear was, "He is not the only one. We have more guests on the way. Soon, they will join him."

As the men walked away, he cast a glance at the camera indicating he knew he was being watched.

"What the hell is going on?" Shekhar asked feeling frustrated with this new development.

"I don't like the looks of this." Sulaiman commented.

"We need to save him. Ajesh, we need to get to him." Shriya said.

"Where is this place? Find the coordinates, quick." Karan asked.

"I have it. Let us move." Said Jenny.

However, as the group was about to leave, the doors locked up and they were unable to get out.

"What just happened?" Shekhar asked.

"Where do you think you are going?" A voice was heard and the group started looking till their eyes fell on a screen. The group came closer each trying to recognize the person.

"I take it that you are trying to recognize who I am but let me explain that my anger towards BASE is an old one. Much more older than the time you may all have joined BASE.. or The Nationalist Corp. We... have time so let me explain my story.

I am Dr. Gomes; I was the lead scientist in BASE and was responsible for research and development of weapons and other ordinance that BASE utilizes. The weapons that you carry were designed by me but I notice they have been modified as per time and requirements. Let me guess, Dr. Prakash, I see.

I... designed... a new biological weapon that could eradicate any enemy threat in a matter of seconds. If utilized, there would have been no one to question BASE but General Bakshi was against it. He feared that it could result in massive loss of lives. He was dead against it but I couldn't allow my years of experiments and research go waste. I had to show him the worth of that weapon... my worth to the world.

It was one of those missions where an army of security elites were deployed to capture/kill an anti-nationalist big shot. I felt that it would be a waste to see elites die in vain if things go south. I decided to use my experiment to make short work of this mission.

I used a drone to transport the weapon to the specific spot. I knew I couldn't do it from BASE towers, so I conducted this 'small experiment' of mine from home. I got to know where the location of the mission was and reached there. I used the drone to locate the big shot and found him. Before, the soldiers could go reach him, I dropped the bomb.

I jumped with joy as the weapon exploded releasing poisonous gases into the room and I knew no one could survive that but something different happened. I didn't expect this. The bomb did not kill them. Instead, the gases entered the body of the people and reacted with the cells in their body converting them... converting them into, what you call them now, Ruts.

The poisonous gases faded away... no, actually, they got absorbed, assimilated into the bodies of the anti-nationals. I watched in horror as the mindless ruts ran towards the security elites. There were 20 of them and the security elites, 50 of them but the latter were of no match. It was a massacre, blood strewn all over the place... the sight of it all... I still get nightmares.

I was the reason for their death. I quivered in fear realizing that I would not be spared. BASE would find me and sentence me to death. All my life of doing service to the nation, all gone in vain for creating this... this... organisms that knew only one thing, to kill and devour. I had no other choice but to escape but not until 4 men, anti-nationals came out of nowhere in a carrier and pulled me into it.

I was knocked out and regained consciousness in a bunker. I didn't know for how long I was out but when I woke up, I was greeted by a man wearing a mask. No, not CODE RED. Someone else, someone you all know but I won't reveal everything now. He called himself CODE GREEN. 'Dr. Gomes, pleased to meet you.'

I didn't answer for I was still trying to cope up with what I had created.

'My men are angry. Can't blame them for you created something that was... how to put it, how to really put it... was horrifying, real horrifying but, it was beautiful. IT... WAS... BEAUTIIFUL.' CODE GREEN was laughing hysterically when explaining the massacre.

He came forward, dragged his chair, sat on it and looked straight into my eyes. He said, 'Don't stop. No, you cannot stop. You have to create this. I will give you anything you want. You will have everything in your disposal to 're-create this magic on a grand scale'.'

The moment he said that, 2 men came in and placed a crate in front of me and walked away.

'Just an advance. You help me and I will give you... what BASE cannot give you. Get your mind clear and tell me your decision.' Saying, CODE GREEN walked out of the room.

I was still shivering. I didn't understand what to do. As I wiped the sweat from my forehead, my eyes fell on the crate. I opened it and I was shocked. Stacks of money, I have never seen so much. I was getting a salary for my work but these people were offering me riches. My mind was cleared in a jiffy.

This time I was laughing hysterically. I couldn't believe what was happening. My world change in a span of few hours. There was no going back. I already walked into a path of darkness and all I could do is to wait for my end... but not before watching the world burn, not before creating something unbelievable.

It was 3 and half years back when I unveiled the first prototype of THE RUT. That is also the time when I got introduced to CODE RED who was tasked to help me with the success of the project, the prototype. CODE RED wanted the ruts to be in our control and that was only possible if we molded them that way. They were trained to live and hunt like dogs. They were even sent on missions with the corp to get a feel of living and hunting in packs.

Soon, we were hearing reports from several news channels and print media of several people encountering mysterious giant rats but BASE had no info about it. Maybe they had but I know BASE too well, especially General Bakshi, who had the habit of keeping everything classified but not for long. CODE RED and I were happy with this info and the former decided to pull the final pin.

'We need to go for the kill. These ruts are ready to cause mayhem. We need a location though. We need a place where we will have complete control of how the battle executes and when to move in/move out.' CODE RED stated.

I thought hard and then remembered this chemical plant.

'I know a place. A chemical plant, there are several underground tunnels where the ruts could be sent in to cause trouble. Once enough trouble... and death is caused, it is imperative that BASE would step in to clear this. We will have our own ruts and in turn, we will release more of the gas converting the security elites into ruts. Mayhem, double mayhem... INFINITE MAYHEM.' I said, and CODE RED applauded my idea.

My idea was set in motion and one by one, the way I envisioned, it came true. I watched as soldier after soldier died either to the ruts or to the gas. BASE's tech was obsolete in terms of handling the poisonous gas released and on top of it, the ruts were wreaking havoc. BASE did not stand a chance. Everything was going well when suddenly, something strange happened.

BASE unveiled a tech that turned the tide of this war. I watched as the new tech, once activated, killed the ruts by destroying the new cells created due to my bio-weapon. My weapon was no more effective as one after the other the ruts fell and soon, the war was over. CODE RED was furious and so was I. We had to fall back on our plan and create something new.

'CODE RED, I know you are angry but please hear me out.' I said as CODE RED was watching the news where General Bakshi was applauding the efforts of the BASE soldiers and also, mourning the loss of those who lost their lives.

'We were so close. We could have won, Gomes. I would have been standing there applauding our efforts over the dead bodies of BASE soldiers.' CODE RED said.

'Who ever said the war is over? It has only begun.' I responded.

CODE RED switched off the TV and then turned towards me.

'You are gifted, CODE RED but also quite young... but I have experience. I may not be a warrior like you but no doubt, I have seen the world a bit more than you.' I spoke.

CODE RED got up from his seat, walked towards me and stood beside me as I looked at a RUT sleeping peacefully inside a glass tank.

'I know General Bakshi. If you listened closely, he did not reveal everything. This mission and all its secrets, like every other major mission, will be made confidential. It will be hidden from everyone's eyes. No one will get to know the actual detail except us.

We will rise again. This mission may haunt a lot of people for years to come but I will make their worst fears come true by creating a new variant. People will quiver in fear and so will BASE.

Your soldiers need you so your only job would be to keep motivating them. Use your anger to lead them and not abuse them. I will do my part in providing the tech that will drive them and their future.

CODE RED... Son... I am there with you so do not lose hope. Instead, think about getting a new lab. A bigger one. We have work to do.' I said as CODE RED stared at me in wonder.

Slowly, a smile appeared on his face. Nodding in agreement, he walked away from the place while my mind started making calculations for a new variant... a new plan. Ladies and Gentlemen, the plan has been set in motion and you will be the first 'SUBJECTS' to see the same. Alas, you may not survive long to see this. So sorry." Dr. Gomes completed his monologue and at that very moment, the group could hear high pitched squealing voices.

"The tanks, they are opening." Sulaiman alerted everyone.

There were 50 tanks in that room and all of them were opening at once. The ruts were awoken and were now looking to feed. Their eyes fell on the control room and they charged towards it. The glasses on the sealed doors and the entire room were strong but not for long.

"Weapons ready people and keep track of your ammo." Karan ordered and the others aimed their weapons.

Jenny was the first to notice something.

"Karan, automated turrets. We need to use them." Jenny announced.

"Find the controls, people. Find the damn controls." Karan ordered.

It didn't take time as Shekhar was quick to find it. He rushed forward and clicked it, the turrets were activated and started firing at the ruts.

"Everybody duck. On the ground or we will be caught in the firing." Shekhar yelled and everybody followed through.

The firing continued for close to 3 minutes as ruts after ruts kept falling to the ground dead. One of the ruts, however, broke through the glass and pounced on Karan.

"KARAN." Jenny shrieked in horror as the rut lunged at Karan's neck but the latter was trying to guard it with his hands.

The others tried to fire but feared that they might hurt Karan too. Karan, however, was not giving up as he grabbed at his dagger on his chest and repeatedly stabbed at the rut's guts. After multiple stabs, the rut was dead and collapsed on the floor. The others rushed in and helped Karan get up on the floor. Karan was not convinced as he took out his handgun and fired all the bullets on the rut's head.

"They are strong, no doubt. We should have brought stronger weapons if we had the slightest of idea what we were going to be up against." Karan commented.

"I... beg to differ, Karan. You should know that I escaped from them. Our assault rifle is powerful, I took down 2 ruts with it. We... never had the chance to utilize them well." Jenny stated.

Karan and the others looked at her.

"BASE had won against the rut problem. I believe Dr. Prakash had not only invented a new tech to deal with the gas but also modified these weapons to… counter the ruts." Sulaiman theorized.

"We will get our chance. Now hurry and find Dr. Gomes. He must be real shocked seeing us survive this. We need to find Darshan too." Said Karan.

The others acknowledge and hurried outside from the control room to the location of the giant tank.

CHAPTER FIVE

THE NEW VARIANT

The group reached the area where the giant tank was located. It was a giant lab with lot of equipment. They stared at the giant tank, confused, due to the huge number of pipes attached to it.

"What is inside this tank?" Asked Shriya.

"We... are not going to like the answer. Trust me." Sulaiman answered.

"So, you people have survived?" It was Dr. Gomes, his voice blaring through the loudspeakers around the lab.

Karan and Jenny spotted the control room on top and they could see Dr. Gomes looking at them.

"Surprised!? Not my fault and no way I am going to take all the credit. The people with me... they are awesome and you are up against all of us." Said Karan.

"You people are like pricks. CODE RED was right about you people. He is having a hard time dealing with you but I will make it easy for him. You are all going to die." Saying, Dr. Gomes clicked a button and the people could see a mid-size tank opening up revealing a rut inside it.

"Here we go again." Shekhar commented.

The rut was released and it came out of the tank. The people were quick to notice that the rut was taller than the usual ones they encountered. Shriya, however, noticed something else.

"No, NO... it can't be. You... YOU MONSTER... WHAT HAVE YOU DONE TO HIM?" Shriya shrieked in horror and grief.

The others were confused but Ajesh was the one who understood. He saw the locket on the neck of the rut. It was a gift from Shriya... a gift... to Darshan.

"Darshan!? DARSHAN... what the hell!?" Ajesh reacted and the others gasped.

"My new creation! Love it?" Dr. Gomes asked sarcastically.

Darshan walked towards the group; he was breathing heavily indicating that he was in pain due to the conversion. It was still not clear whether he was in control or not.

"He is still untrained so I am not sure what would be the result. Once he is trained, he will be the forerunner of the new variants that will unleash hell and guarantee victory." Dr. Gomes stated as he marveled over his creation much to the disturbance of the group.

Shriya walked forwards towards Darshan.

"Shriya, what are you doing? Don't be stupid. Stay away from it." Jenny tried to stop her.

"Shriya, listen to me. He is not what he is." Ajesh tried but Shriya did not heed.

Karan aimed his rifle and the others reluctantly followed.

"Ajesh, if there is a slight chance of saving him, we will do our best but I cannot guarantee anything." Karan said.

Ajesh did not answer but he understood what Karan was trying to explain.

"Darshan, I know you are in there. Please, listen to me. We will save you. Stay with us. Don't give up. Please don't give in." Shriya said trying to pacify Darshan.

Darshan looked hideous but that did not deter Shriya as she touched his face in an effort to comfort him.

"Yes, don't give in. Please. I beg of you. You are my brother and I won't leave you. We will never leave you." Shriya said again.

Just when it looked like things were in control, Darshan let out a loud roar and brought his fists up to smash Shriya but Shekhar was already prepared for that. He ran, pushed Shriya aside and with a click of a button, a shield appeared that took the blow of Darshan's fist. Shekhar was pushed back but he held his ground.

Darshan continued to roar and jumped up high in the air that shocked the group.

"Scatter. Stay away from his sight. Find a hiding place." Karan signaled and everyone heeded.

As the group scattered in time, Darshan slammed on the ground wrecking a part of it.

"What has Dr. Gomes done to him?" Shriya asked.

"This is a test of survival. Switch on the timer. I am going to enjoy this." Dr. Gomes commented.

Darshan turned around to look for the group but they were in hiding. He started to smell the air to catch their scent.

"Of course, he is an animal now. We cannot stay hidden for now. He will find us." Shekhar commented in a low tone.

"There must be a way. A way to subdue him. We cannot... we cannot kill him. That is not an option." Ajesh stated.

"Killing is the last option, Ajesh but I am sorry, we may have to. As for subduing him, we do not have that 'technology'. We didn't think that we would have to fight against mindless monsters." Karan said.

Darshan came closer and Shekhar quickly signaled to change cover. Meanwhile, Sulaiman had an idea.

"If we can lure Darshan into a tank, we can activate it and sterilize him. Not only will he be trapped but also, the mechanism in the tank will calm him down." Sulaiman said.

"You want to play tag with him. He is not in his senses and he is hell bent on killing us." Jenny commented.

"And what if... he is lured in? What next? How can we save him?" Shriya asked.

Suddenly, they heard a roar. Darshan found them behind a row of equipment. They scurried in time as Darshan smashed the area. Sulaiman decided to take the chance as he rushed towards a tank, stood in front of it and aimed his rifle at Darshan.

"Come on, Darshan. Come to me." Saying, Sulaiman fired his rifle in the air to draw his attention.

Darshan was drawn towards the firing and he slowly walked towards Sulaiman.

"He is crazy. What the hell is he thinking?" Karan asked shocked.

"He is trying to lure Darshan into that tank. To sterilize him." Jenny answered.

Darshan was now close to Sulaiman and the latter was preparing himself to step aside just in time to lure Darshan in but he was in for a surprise.

"Please... just... kill... me." Darshan spoke up and everyone there froze in shock and horror.

"Please... I beg... of... you. I... don't want... to... kill you. I am... in pain. I... am... not... in control. Don't put me... into that... thing... again. Kill me... please." Darshan knelt down close to the barrel of Sulaiman's rifle.

Dr. Gomes was also surprised with this development and got up from his seat.

"Now that was unexpected. I know I created a new and intelligent variant but did not know he was this intelligent." Dr. Gomes commented.

The others walked up to Darshan who was breathing heavily now. They could see him crying, he was in pain and pleaded to the group to end the suffering.

"I... am... sorry. I didn't... want to... attack. I... wanted you... to fire... at me. Kill... me. You... cannot... allow this. That... monster... cannot win. I will... I will..." Darshan looked at the group and then looked at the control room where Dr. Gomes was standing and watching.

"Do me... a favor... Shriya, I... love you. I am... proud... of you... I am... sorry I... couldn't give... you the... life that you... deserved... but BASE will... protect you.... Major... will protect... you. I am... sorry... for this..." Saying, Darshan let out a blood curdling roar and jumped over the group.

Confused, the group looked on but not until they realized Darshan's intention.

"Darshan, don't... COME BACK." Shriya cried out but to no avail.

Darshan was heading towards the control room which shocked Dr. Gomes.

"What is going on? Why is he coming here? This was not a part of the plan." Dr. Gomes stepped back as the menacing form of Darshan was approaching the control room.

Dr. Gomes quickly activated the turrets around the area and had them aimed at Darshan. The turrets started to fire. Darshan cried out in pain as he was mercilessly shot but he did not stop as he slammed through the windows of the control room and pounced on Dr. Gomes.

The group could now hear the loud cries of the scientist. A cry of shock, anger, pain and sadness, a cry that could only be heard when a person least expected a turn of events that could shatter his dreams and his hopes. The turrets stopped firing and the room fell silent.

Shriya was the first to run towards the control room.

"Shriya, wait... the turrets." Saying, Ajesh ran behind her.

The others were quick to notice that the turrets were all down.

"They are programmed to kill the ruts. Not us. Gomes would have programmed it otherwise but, I guess, it is too late for him now." Jenny stated.

"Let us check on Darshan. Move it, people. Quick." Karan ordered, as they rushed towards the control center.

When they reached, they could see Darshan lying on a pool of blood. Shriya was crying profusely while Ajesh sat beside her and looked on. They also could see Dr. Gomes, shredded to pieces. Not the first time they saw anything like this but they cannot deny that it was still a disturbing sight.

"He is not going to make it. The turrets got him real bad." Shekhar said.

Darshan was still moving but was groaning in pain. He noticed Karan and the others.

"Major, get... them... out of... here." Darshan tried to speak up.

"We are getting you out of here." Karan tried to re-assure though he knew it was too late for him.

"No, leave me... here. Get out... of... here. There is... something... else. Something... worse." Saying, Darshan breathed his last.

A heartbroken Shriya hugged the lifeless body of Darshan and wailed loudly. At that very moment, the others spotted Sulaiman activating a terminal and looking at it. They moved closer to him to check. A recorded video started playing on the terminal.

"The prototype is ready, Doctor. Need your authorization to activate the same." An AI was communicating with Dr. Gomes.

"When the right time comes, I will have it activated. Keep it in standby mode for now." Dr. Gomes responded.

"Acknowledged." The AI said.

After a few minutes, Dr. Gomes spoke up, "I am not sure if my time has come but I am not going to give the world the satisfaction to taste victory over my defeat. In case... In case, I die, activate the prototype. If not while I am alive, I will watch the world get eaten up from hell. It will, no doubt, be a sight to behold."

The AI acknowledged with a beep. The video ended and the group looked at each other. That very moment, tremors were felt followed by a rumbling sound and then... a bloodcurdling roar.

"We need to get out of here. This isn't over yet. Run. Get out of here." Karan ordered and the others followed.

Ajesh grabbed Shriya and dragged her out of the control room. As the group left the room, Karan and Shekhar glanced back to see the tank open up and reveal the secret inside. They looked at it, horrified. The rumbling was going strong and it knocked back the duo from their senses as they fled from the place. The group did not stop for anything as they came back to the area, they were holding the interrogation.

"Guys, look. The storm, it has faded." Jenny stated.

"Sulaiman, prep the ship. We are leaving. Whatever that thing is we saw... we need to stop it. We need to warn BASE." Karan said in a panic tone.

"What are you talking about? What did you see?" Sulaiman asked.

"Later, idiot. We need to run. Move people, to the ship." Karan exclaimed running towards where the ship was docked.

"The storm. Have you noticed? It has stopped. When did this happen?" Jenny asked.

"Looks like the storm knew that we have bigger issues to deal with." Shekhar commented.

As they got into the ship, Sulaiman advised everyone to wear the seat belts and started the engines.

"BASE to Trident Squad, this is General Bakshi. Anybody read me?" It was Gen. Bakshi on the radio.

"Radio is functioning. Good timing. I will handle this. You get the bird in the air." Karan said.

Clearing his voice, he spoke up again, "Sir, we got the 'package' but we have an issue. Dr. Gomes, remember him."

There was a slight delay before Gen. Bakshi spoke up, "Story of my life. Someone always comes back – either from the unknown or from a heap of classified files. I remember that name, kid but you better give me the good news."

"Well, sir... the good news is that he is dead. Killed by his own minion." Karan replied.

"Now, wait a minute!? What are you blabbering about!?" The General asked in an irritated voice.

That very moment, there was a huge explosion and the group could see a huge ball of smoke and dust but within the dust, they could see a silhouette of a monster with red glaring eyes.

"As if it was not already a bad day." Jenny commented.

"Nah, this is the probably going to be the best day of our lives." Shekhar responded.

"Oh really. That is one 50-60 ft of 'Doomsday' out of there and you are debating about whether this is a good day or a bad day." Ajesh retorted.

Karan had seen it and now it was the turn of BASE to see to it.

"Sir, we also have a bad day, I mean... news. You may want to see this." Saying, Karan signaled Sulaiman to start streaming the situation to BASE command.

Everyone in BASE command watched in horror as the monster came out of the dust and smoke, and with a loud roar charged behind the carrier. General Bakshi, however, was expressionless.

"Well, what are you waiting for? Sound the alarm and send re-enforcement. No way that thing is coming towards the city." The General ordered.

Back to the carrier, the group noticed something else that was waiting for them.

"Of course, it is the anti-nationals. What is there to be surprised about? They were lying in wait to pounce on us once the storm would clear but they are in for a surprise." Sulaiman commented.

The anti-nationals had a battalion in place with 3 scavengers. The soldiers were alarmed and horrified at this new development. Their guns were aimed at the carrier but they quickly adjusted their aim.

"Well, let us see if our 'old friends' are a match for that. I am open to bets." The General commented.

The anti-nationals started firing at the monster while the carrier flew over them.

"They are not firing at us." A surprised Sulaiman stated.

"Wow, you surely look disappointed. Turn around if you want them to." Jenny commented and Sulaiman sneered at her.

The anti-nationals were no match to the monster as the latter destroyed the scavengers and killed the rest. It then set its eyes on the carrier.

"No doubt, it will follow us. Its sole purpose is to kill or destroy." Ajesh said.

"We cannot allow it to follow us. If it hits the city, then it will lead to mayhem. 1000s of people will lose their lives." Shekhar said.

Sulaiman looked at the tracker and found something.

"Guys, there is a mine a few clicks from here. Looks huge. We can lure it there." Sulaiman suggested.

Karan had a look at the tracker and then to the direction of the mine.

"This is an active mine and is also close to... an active volcano!?" Karan was truly astonished.

"I have heard of this mine and the risk the people take working over here. It is also said to be quite an interesting mine as all possible minerals required for the functioning of the city are available there. The risk the people take to mine those resources is worth mentioning considering it is next to an active volcano that has not exploded in the last 50 years." Jenny explained.

Karan thought hard. He had to take a decision and he had to take it fast.

"Last 50 years, eh!? Not sure if the waiting ends today but we have no choice. Into the mine. Alert the people in the mine and also, alert BASE of our... plan." Karan said.

"Plan? What plan? What kind of plan!?" Sulaiman asked.

"I don't know. I... just tell them. Say anything." Karan said to a bewildered Sulaiman.

"Ajesh, Shriya, off with the existing suits and armor up. Grab a weapon. This fight is on." Karan ordered.

"Sure is, Major. Besides, Darshan needs to be avenged." Ajesh responded.

"Everyone who died because of this madness... needs to be avenged. And it happens today." Said Karan and the others acknowledged.

"Sulaiman, have they all been alerted?" Karan asked.

"Yes, the mine is being evacuated. BASE is on high alert but the General is asking what is the plan." Sulaiman answered.

"Just tell him to send the back up to the mine. In case, we fail... though failure is not an option at the moment." Karan said.

Jenny decided to communicate the same while Sulaiman flew the carrier towards the mine at the top speed with the monster running behind them. They could hear the sirens blaring which meant that the evacuation was in process.

"It won't be completed in time and the worst part of it, we may not be able to save all of them." Jenny stated.

"The dark side of our job, Jenny. Nothing we can do now. Killing this monster is important. We may lose a few lives but we can save millions at the same time. Bring out the floor plan of the mine. Eyes open, people. All of you. We need an idea to bring this thing down." Karan said.

A hologram of the mine appeared in the middle of the ship. Sulaiman flew the carrier through the mine cave and located a place to land the carrier away from the eyes of the monster.

"We need to stay away from the monster's vision and I found a place for the same. Enough time for you guys to devise a plan." Sulaiman said and the other acknowledged.

The mine was huge. Only a few people remained while the rest had probably been evacuated through a back door. There were a few unlucky souls who came in contact with the monster and got killed. Some of them were in hiding. Sulaiman continued to fly on and soon reached the landing pad which was situated about 300 ft above a huge open area filled with molten lava falls. As the group came out of the carrier, they could make out 6 falls though there could be more of them.

"It is really hot in here. How do people work here?" Jenny asked.

"They have special suits that keep their body warm. The hard part is that they have to constantly check that their suit is not ruptured or damaged. One small rupture and they have to go back and get it sorted. Otherwise, they are dead.

What is amazing is that this mine has been running for 30 years and there have been only 4 casualties. This is only because they have a special unit that constantly checks that the suits of the staff do not get damaged. They have cameras installed giving them that information and once they detect it, they immediately request the worker to report to them." Shekhar explained.

"Team work makes the dream work. Moral of the story." Sulaiman commented.

"All right, people. General knowledge class over. Time for action. Where is the monster?" Karan asked.

A roar was heard that very moment which indicated that the monster was close by.

"He is around the corner. ETA 10 minutes." Shekhar answered.

"This area is open. There is no one here except us. This is where we need to hold the monster until back up arrives. However, no way in hell we can hold that thing for long. We need a plan now." Saying, Karan brought out the hologram of the mine on his wrist monitor.

"Karan, we are... we are directly below the mountain. Which mean... there is lava either flowing over us or accumulated over us." Jenny stated.

"You mean if we drill holes on the ceiling, the lava will drop over us." Ajesh added.

"Or will drop on the monster if we are able to hold it here." Karan added to the comments while looking at the ceiling.

"Wait, is that even possible? No way we can drill holes. It will take years before we crack that ceiling." Shekhar responded.

Karan thought hard while another roar was heard indicating again that the monster was getting closer.

"How strong is the firepower of this carrier?" Karan asked.

"It is substantial but if you are thinking of using it to blow the ceiling, it will still take time. We are talking about distracting the monster while we shoot up the ceiling." Sulaiman answered.

"Unless, maybe we can use that." Everyone looked at Shekhar who was looking at something else. A giant driller and excavator.

"There are 2 of them. We can use them but there is still a risk. We may be able to drill but soon the ceiling will turn fragile and collapse with the lava. We may not be able to escape in time." Said Shriya.

"We all signed up for this. We need to take the risk. Stay focused, the first chance of escape and we take it without hesitation. Listen up, sulaiman as usual you are flying the ship and Ajesh, you are on the turret. The job for both of you is to keep the monster distracted while myself, Shekhar, Jenny and Shriya, we are aboard

the excavators. Shriya, stick with Shekhar. Jenny, you are with me."
Karan explained the plan.

The others nodded in acknowledgement.

"I believe you have no questions. Good, for honestly, I do not
have an answer to any of them. Sulaiman, how long till back up
arrives?" Karan asked.

"20 minutes." Sulaiman answered.

"May God bless us all. Everyone, get to work." Said Karan.

CHAPTER SIX

ONBOARDED

The 2 teams on the excavator started to drill the ceiling while Sulaiman and Ajesh were on the carrier hidden and lying-in wait.

"Back up arriving in 5 minutes. They should have been over here already." Sulaiman commented.

"Patience, comrade. Even if they do reach, they have to follow a path that is not straight. I hope the psionics reach first." Karan said.

"What is a psionic?" Shriya asked.

"Fighter planes. Medium sized that carry 2 pilots. Their firepower is powerful and lethal." Shekhar answered.

Shriya was quite for a long time, sad and depressed due to Darshan's death. The word 'fighter planes' was like a magic word that brought a smile on her face.

"I always wanted to ride one of those. I would have love to become a pilot... if things were different in my life." Shriya said.

Unaware to her, her radio was switched on and everyone heard it.

"So, we have a competition, Sulaiman. How about you give the seat to her when this is over?" Jenny spoke up.

Shriya was at first taken aback but then giggled.

"A lady pilot!? No way." Sulaiman feigned a sneer while saying that.

"Oh really! You hear that, Shriya. He is challenging us." Jenny said.

"I have heard that woman pilots in BASE are a class apart. Would love to be a part of that team. If Sulaiman sir agrees to train me though." Shriya said, she was slowly starting to open up.

"We loved going to the arcade and our first pick was always the flying simulator. Shriya, Darshan and myself would always compete with each other and every time, Shriya would win. I have seen you fly; Sulaiman and you are good. However, being in favor of my friend, Jenny is right. You have a competition." Ajesh said.

"We will see about that, Ajesh. Let us safely get you all to BASE." Sulaiman responded.

That very moment, the group could hear loud thuds. Footsteps, followed by a loud roar.

"Here it comes." Karan said.

And sure enough, the monster arrived. Slowly and steadily, it walked into the center of the mine and was sniffing the air. Without a doubt, it could hear the drilling noise and slowly, looked up.

"Peek-a-boo." Shekhar commented.

The monster let out a loud roar at the drillers. It started to look around for ways to climb up but was intelligent enough to notice the lava falls.

"It is looking for a way to climb up. Sulaiman, time to dance. Keep it distracted. We are a few feet into flooding this place with lava but we need the time.

Sulaiman acknowledged and looked at Ajesh, who also nodded in acknowledgement. The former powered up the engines and flew towards the monster, and started firing seemingly annoying it.

"Hits are getting registered, Sulaiman. It is not hard skinned as it looks." Ajesh stated.

"Good news, I guess. Let us bring it down. This thing doesn't need to exist." Sulaiman said.

Soon, the ceiling was starting to crack up and little by little, molten lava was falling from the ceiling.

"Sulaiman, be careful. The ceiling has started to crack." Karan said.

Sulaiman noticed as the ceiling was given way.

"I will take care. You guys need to get out of there. Stay too long and you will get engulfed in it." Sulaiman warned.

Jenny noticed that the driller was losing its hold on the ceiling as it was weakening.

"Sulaiman is right. Karan, we need to move. The ceiling has loosened up. We better attach explosives and get away from the blast radius." Jenny stated.

Karan looked at the ceiling and heeded Jenny's advice.

"Shekhar, plant the explosives. We need to leave now." Karan said.

Shekhar acknowledged and the explosives were planted on the ceiling. However, a mishap occurred. The monster was wounded but still standing and Sulaiman could make out that they were low on firepower to bring it down.

"Where the hell is the support? What is taking them so long?" Ajesh reacted.

The monster cast his eyes on the driller that Shekhar and Shriya were in. It grabbed a rock and hurled it at the driller. The rock found its mark as one of the engines exploded and the driller was on a free fall.

"Oh no, Shekhar." Jenny reacted as Karan looked on.

"Shriya, grab on to something." Shekhar shouted.

The driller crashed against a wall and then hit the ground hard.

"Shriya. Goddamit. Sulaiman, we need to get them out of there." Ajesh said.

Shekhar and Shriya were alive but were wounded. Shekhar, however, was able to get up on his feet. He checked on Shriya but not until his eyes fell on the monster that was coming towards the driller.

"Really!? You wanna fight me. Alright. Man to beast, eye to eye." Saying, Shekhar grabbed his weapon, activated grenade mode and started firing at the monster.

The monster came close and was about to devour Shekhar when Karan, out of desperation slammed the driller he was controlling on to the head of the monster. The force was too much to bear, while the monster was taken aback and moved away from the point, Karan lost control of the driller and it too crashed onto the ground.

"That was insane." Jenny commented.

Karan clutched his head and then looked out. The monster was still stunned. The ceiling was already cracked up and molten lava was slowly and steadily falling from all directions. Karan then looked at the explosives on the driller and then looked at the monster. He then looked at Jenny who was wincing in pain.

Karan punched some buttons on the monitor of the driller which activated all the explosives. He then set the timer, made his way back to Jenny and carried her out of the driller. He tried his best to get to a safe distance, he looked back to see the monster back to its senses and looking menacingly at Karan. It let out a loud growl and rushed towards Karan but not before the driller exploded in a huge ball of flame. Karan and Jenny were thrown backwards due to the impact and so was Shekhar who did not expect it.

The explosion burnt the skin of the monster who roared in excruciating pain. The earth shook due to the explosion, Sulaiman and Ajesh observed as the monster fell with a thud and was motionless.

'I think we got it. Let us get them and get out of here before we get trapped here." Said Sulaiman and Ajesh acknowledged.

Sulaiman landed the carrier and Ajesh rushed to the aid of Shekhar and Shriya while Sulaiman headed towards Karan and Jenny. As the group moved back towards the carrier, the monster growled again. The group looked back in horror as the creature slowly got up.

'Woah, it is angry. Very angry." Shekhar commented.

Karan looked at the monster with a grim look and then looked at the ceiling. The explosives were primed and ready. Push of a button and the whole place will be flooded with molten lava engulfing everything and everyone in this area. He raised the remote, finger on the button and the others saw it. He did it intentionally so that the others knew of his next move, the last resort.

"Do it, Karan. Do it now. We are with you on this." Shekhar said.

Karan took a deep breath and looked at the monster that was close enough. He was about to click the button when suddenly, the group saw 2 missiles flying from the left, the missiles found their mark as the monster bellowed in pain from the impact.

"Trident squad. We are here. Let us take care of this bastard." Said the squadron leader.

"Psionics." Shriya spoke up.

The psionics pounded the monster with missiles and laser fire till the latter was down and out. It groaned in pain, it tried to lift its body but couldn't.

"Everyone, on the carrier." Karan ordered and others followed.

Sulaiman started the engines and flew the carrier out at top speed.

"Karan, do it. Do it now." Shekhar said.

Karan heeded and pressed the button. Boom sounds were heard followed by the loud crashing sounds indicating that the ceiling had collapsed. Molten lava flooded the area, the monster was in no shape to move as it let out a roar with its last breath as he was engulfed in the molten lava.

Sulaiman's carrier and the psionics escaped from the area as the automatic lockdown was initiated. The group could make out giant doors closing.

"So, they knew that there was molten lava on that ceiling and that is why they created this lockdown? Clever, real clever." Jenny stated.

The carrier and the jets escaped from the area. News reached BASE and other cities around the planet that the monster was successfully defeated. The General and his team were waiting for the trident squad to return.

Sulaiman brought out a notepad, wrote 5 on it and then put it back.

"What was that for?" Karan asked.

"5th time in 4 years of our career that the General has come out to receive us. It is going to be quite a story when I retire. Better, when I have kids who need to know that their daddy is a hero." Said Sulaiman and chuckled at that comment.

"Call me pessimistic but trouble always seem to follow us. Call ourselves lucky that we get out of it unscathed. Only God knows for how long." Saying, Karan walked towards the back of the carrier and opened the door.

The others looked on and then looked at each other.

"Trust me, he is the most optimistic guy around town. It is I who ends up being pessimistic but he has faced issues more than anyone so you may find him being morbid sometime." Shekhar tried to defend Karan.

"I know, Shekhar. There are still a lot of things he has not revealed about himself. I only know that he has never seen his father and he has been missing since his birth. He knows nothing about his mother too. I am patiently waiting for the day when he is truly open with me. For now, let him be. We are with him." Jenny said as she looked at Karan and smiled.

Shekhar chuckled and commented, "I feel so insecure now. You are taking my place once and for all."

Jenny stared at Shekhar confused but she was quick to realize what he meant. She smirked and said, "Don't worry. Poorna is the replacement. It is not like Karan is your boyfriend or something. Even if he was, sorry, he is... taken."

Everyone burst out laughing hearing that comment much to the surprise of Karan who turned back to see what was going on. The carrier landed and the group came out of it.

"Trident squad. As always you have done the impossible but it was a big risk you took to take on the monster which just a few people." The General stated.

"Agreed but we had no choice. We couldn't let the monster hit the city and wreak havoc. It is either that or we risk losing a lot of lives." Said Karan.

The General then looked at the defected individuals. Karan turned around and asked them to come forward.

"Sir, they proved their loyalty along with their bravery. They helped us escape, helped us fight the monster and made sure that we all come out alive." Karan explained.

"The Major here is generous. Honestly, it was supposed to be a rescue mission but we got involved. Perhaps, yes, an opportunity and we do stay true to our words." Said Ajesh.

"I see only 2 of you. Where is the 3rd?" The General asked.

Shriya looked down, she felt pained but Jenny consoled her. Ajesh also was speechless; he had forgotten all of it for sometime.

"Sir, Darshan... Shriya's brother died while trying to help us fight the monster. He fought bravely and gave up his life." Karan explained.

Ajesh stared at Karan, he wanted to say something but Shekhar coaxed him to remain silent along with signaling that it was ok. Ajesh remained silent and nodded in agreement.

The General was a man of experience. He understood that they were hiding something but this was the Trident Squad, he knew that it was necessary and pretended to believe it. The Major General, however, wanted to have his say.

"This doesn't change the fact that they are anti-nationals. They have blood on their hands. They have killed our soldiers. One right does not clear out all the wrongs. Men, arrest them." The Major General said.

The soldiers behind the Major General came forward but Karan's squad members came forward and in a show of courage and willpower pointed their weapons at the soldiers.

"How dare you!? This is treason. This is an act of insubordination. I can have you all court martial-ed." The Major General shouted but the trident squad did not budge.

Karan showed his side of fury, something which he rarely showed but when he did, it was a not a good sign, "Sir, pray that I never show my act of insubordination. You do know my influence so if I resist, you know very well why I would do the same."

The Major General was shocked. He knew the Trident Squad was a well-known and established squad and the world was aware of their success rate. That being said, any sign of hostility against them meant hostility towards the nation itself.

The General was silent for long but now had to speak up.

"Karan, behave yourself and ask your team to stand down." The General ordered.

Karan dared not refuse the General. He ordered his squad to do the same and they heeded.

"Pradeep, you are forgetting the main motive of this mission. It was to bring these people to safety so that they can be interrogated. They agreed to it and defected from the Nationalist Corp. Karan and his team are not liars. Jenny over here has already transmitted the initial interrogation data.

These people are subject to misleading information and deserve a second chance to know the reality. However, understand that the first sign of trouble from you guys and I will immediately order for termination." The General said.

"I understand, Sir. I know people are angry with us and it is normal but be assured that we won't fail you. We have come seeking redemption and in return, you will have all the support and information needed." Ajesh stated.

"Karan, they are our guest and will be treated fairly. They are still your responsibility till we decide the next step. I have already allotted a room for them where they will be monitored. Poorna will guide you there and she will handle further formalities pertaining to this." The General said.

Poorna was standing behind but came forward acknowledging this communication. The trident squad members also acknowledged and took Ajesh and Shriya with them. As everyone dispersed, the General then looked at the Major General.

"Still on to it, Pradeep? Still disbelieving the might of our soldiers? May I ask why?" The General asked.

"The way the trident squad works, they employ unconventional methods. Do you think that is acceptable? That mine is the country's biggest asset and now it is off limits because of their stupidity." The Major General replied.

"What is more important? The mine or the lives of the people. The government is already working on getting it up and running, and it will take 5 days for the same." The General said.

The Major General had no answer to that. He kept silent.

"A lot of officers have invested their money in business ventures and as per rules, it is very much allowed but at the end of the day, we are soldiers. We have a responsibility to the protect the country and its people at all cost. You in particular seemed a lot more interested in the mine. Receiving a lot of profits, I see." The General said.

The Major General was now frowning. He was angry but tried his best to control it, not to show it. The General understood that he had targeted the latter's soft spot. As he started to walk away, he placed his hand on the Major General's shoulder and whispered, "Easy, my friend. We are the experienced bunch. You have secrets but you do not know how to hide them. I, on the other hand, can quickly catch them. I hope whatever you are doing is in your best interest, otherwise it won't take me time to uncover all your secrets."

The General walked away while the Major General looked on.

"I know how to hide secrets; my friend and I challenge you to uncover them." The Major General thought to himself giving a sly smile.

CHAPTER SEVEN

EPILOGUE

Karan was looking at the report that was filed post the complete interrogation of the defected. Without a doubt, his mind was blown with the number of details that the 2 people provided.

"Just 2 people and so much information. Anyone else in our place would have got this published and made billions." Karan commented.

"We can, you know, take permission and have this published. Maybe, BASE will allow us a percentage of commission from the sale." Shekhar said and the others laughed over that.

Karan nodded in denial and said, "Easier said than done, bro."

Ajesh and Shriya had also collected a lot of photos revealing the people involved, assets, armaments, and vehicles. There were also photos of certain areas which BASE had termed classified and off limits but Karan couldn't help wonder as to why.

"They are... beyond the threshold." Sulaiman stated.

"Threshold. And what is that?" Karan asked confused.

"Wait, you don't know? I thought..." Sulaiman started but then looked at everyone else, they were also staring at him in bewilderment.

"Wow, seriously. I am the only one in this group who is totally updated on this." Sulaiman commented.

"You seem to be hanging out either with the right guys or the wrong guys." Karan said.

"Nah, he is hanging out with people who belong to some cult that deals with conspiracy theories." Jenny said, she finished cleaning her rifle. She prayed to it and then placed it inside a container.

"No, no, believe me. It is true. It exists. A whole new world that BASE made off limits. You need special permission. Like, even the General cannot permit the same." Sulaiman tried to explain but no one seem interested, no one except Karan who was looking at a particular photo.

Without informing, he got up from his seat and rushed outside.

"What the hell happened to him?" Shekhar asked.

Jenny was taken aback by this behavior. She then looked at Sulaiman and frowned.

"What!? What did I do!?" Sulaiman asked.

Karan raced towards the General's Office; he took permission from the guards who allowed him in.

"Karan, any problem?" General Bakshi asked.

Karan placed the particular photo on the table and asked, "Find anyone familiar?"

The General looked at the photo closely.

"How did anyone miss this?" Karan asked again.

The General understood, he placed the photo on the table and informed the guards through the intercom to not allow anyone else inside unless it was an emergency. He then activated his wrist monitor and searched through the database. The name of a person appeared and both Karan and the General could see the words – DECEASED – written on it.

"The mole we were talking about, we were searching for so long, this is the one. He is not with us. He is long gone from our organization and we were frantically searching for him while he was busy enjoying and building an army." The General deduced.

"This is a great development but we cannot let this go waste." Karan stated.

"I know. We can create a special team. You can lead it. Track him, find him and bring him to us. You can kill him if you want but our primary intention would be to bring him alive because he is reason that the anti-nationals are ticking." The General said.

"No, that wouldn't work. He is not the only mole. There are others within BASE who are supporting the anti-nationals from the shadows. We need to do something similar and hit them where it hurts, with their weapon." Karan said.

The General understood and wanted to know more as to what Karan was planning.

"Go on, son. What do you want to do? You have my support." The General leaned forward wanting to listen intently.

"Before that, I have a question. What is the 'THRESHOLD'?" Karan asked.

The General was at first taken aback by the question but then took a grip of himself.

He then spoke up, "Not all secrets remain secrets, I see. Some are just travelling around and people consider them as either urban legends or rumors. However, considering the question has come from you... and I don't want to know who passed that info to you... I will tell you everything provided you keep silent about it. Do we have a deal?"

Karan stared at the General and then flashed a sly smile.

TO BE CONTINUED...